Farm Chase

Black Bull Farm

Rod Campbell

PUFFIN

This is the angry bull

who chased the . . .

who chased the . . .

who chased the . . .

who chased the . . .

who chased the ...

who chased the ...

who didn't chase anyone at all ...

but found a nice
cosy corner, curled
up and . . .

Also by Rod Campbell

ABC ZOO
DEAR ZOO
FARM 123
FARM BABIES
NOISY FARM

PUFFIN BOOKS
Published by the Penguin Group: London, New York,
Australia, Canada, India, New Zealand and South Africa
Penguin Books Ltd, Registered Offices:
80 Strand, London WC2R 0RL, England

puffinbooks.com

First published in Puffin Books 2004
4
The moral right of the author/illustrator has been asserted
Made and printed in Malaysia by Tien Wah Press (Pte) Ltd
ISBN-13 978-0-14056-898-1